Mystery-Fold

Stories to Tell, Draw, and Fold

Valerie Marsh

Illustrated by Patrick Luzadder

Published by Alleyside Press, a Division of Freline, Inc.
P. O. Box 889
Hagerstown, MD 21741

ISBN 0-913853-31-3

Printed in the United States of America

I dedicate this book to the many talented storytellers in classrooms everywhere. The names of the characters in these stories represent storytellers I have known.

Contents

Introduction

Why storytelling?

Listening to a story is one of the most effective ways for children to learn a variety of concepts. When children themselves can tell a story, they have mastered many skills in the process. By telling a story, they can learn to integrate verbal language as well as develop critical-thinking skills, sequencing skills, short- and long-term memory skills, and, most importantly, creative imagination. They can learn to distinguish between reality and fantasy, good and bad, funny and sad.

Drawing with markers and folding the paper helps develop fine motor skills. And finally, they can just plain enjoy themselves, escaping from the real world for a few moments and coming back to it with renewed vigor and increased confidence.

What is a Mystery-Fold?

Drawing and folding the "answer" to a story out of a piece of paper is a unique way to tell a story, and it yields an unusual surprise for the listener. It is also a great way for children to learn to tell stories. The stories in this book are short, easy to tell, and deceptively simple. The stories and their corresponding paper-folded pictures are designed to be simple enough for children ages five and up to retell or revise into their own versions. They can be simply enjoyed by children ages three and up.

As you tell these stories, you will be drawing on both the left and right sides of the paper. At the end of the story, the object is completely drawn. During the last sentence of the story, you fold the paper together to reveal the "answer." It will be a surprise because it is not mentioned in the story.

After you tell a few of these stories, your students will soon be telling their own Mystery-Fold tales both at home and at school. Some children will bring stories to school that they have made up at home; this generates enthusiasm in other children to do the same thing. Before you know it, parents also will be involved and looking forward to the Mystery-Fold stories their children learn at school or create themselves.

Why combine storytelling and drawing?

Telling a story while drawing a picture is a great way to completely capture your listeners' interest. This is an unusual approach to story-telling, and, because you fold your picture together at the end of the story—Wow!—you've got a memorable story!

Watching the drawing come to life on paper helps both the storyteller and the listeners remember the steps of the story. The drawing lines are related to the plot, and the picture created by folding the drawing offers the answer or outcome to your story. You do not have to draw freehand; all drawings are traced lightly before telling the story.

Another plus: When speaking in front of a group, most people feel more confident if they have something to do with their hands; the paper and marker fulfill this need.

Most children love to draw and spend lots of time at it. After experiencing a Mystery-Fold story involving a simple drawing, children often will take their own doodles and turn them into a story.

In telling Mystery-Fold stories, children have many opportunities to use the higher order thinking skills. They will comprehend, apply their information, analyze, synthesize, and evaluate in order to understand the Mystery-Fold story you tell and/or to write and tell one of their own.

Do you need to be an artist or seasoned storyteller?

No! All you need to do is trace! The patterns are designed to be used with typing paper. Simply place a piece of typing paper over the pattern and trace over it very lightly in pencil. Since you prefold the paper on all the fold lines, it's easy to fold up again at the end of your story. Use a thick black marker (or other color if it relates to your story) when you are telling the story, and just trace over the pencil lines as your story unfolds!

You do not have to be a great performer either in order to tell a good Mystery-Fold story. Think of yourself as a "storyteacher"— someone who tells stories to children and then helps children themselves become storytellers.

As a storyteacher, you are telling stories not just for entertainment, but also to demonstrate to children how they can do it. This is the main goal: to empower children to tell stories.

When should you tell Mystery-Fold stories?

- **When integrating your curriculum and/or using a whole language approach:**

Science—Tell a story involving an animal to introduce a unit on animals.

Literature—Tell a story that has the same animal in it that the upcoming basal story does. Or choose a story that has the same name as a character in your next story, or some of the same characteristics or problems.

Art—Tell a Mystery-Fold story to introduce folding or drawing techniques.

Listening Skills—You have to listen closely to the story in order to retell or redraw it.

Sequencing Skills—What comes first, second, last, etc., in the story?

Writing Skills—Write or outline the steps of your story.

- **When celebrating or rewarding a group of children:**

Birthdays—Choose an appropriate story and change the name of the main character to that of the birthday person.

Parties—Tell a Mystery-Fold story at a holiday party.

Rewards—Children need to learn that rewards can take forms other than material things such as food, stickers, etc. Rewards can also be active entertainment rather than passive (such as a movie).

- **When keeping children entertained and occupied:**

Quiet times after recess.

Waiting times between classes or during lunch periods.

Unexpected delays such as waiting for a late speaker during a school convocation.

Entertainment at a school fair or carnival.

After-school art and crafts programs.

After-school child-care programs.

How to tell Mystery-Fold stories

1. Drawing steps are related to the story. As the character goes places or does something, you add a new line to your picture.

2. First place a piece of white paper over the pattern in the book. With a pencil, trace all

drawing lines very lightly. Mark where you will place the tape. (Later on, you might let your listeners in on this secret.)

Some stories involve a previously drawn picture that is revealed at the end of the story. Go ahead and draw this in with your marker. If the marker shows through your paper, you might want to use a thicker paper or a lighter marker.

3. Practice telling each story while drawing so that it becomes natural to talk and draw at the same time. Becoming familiar with the story and the drawing allows you to present the story easily and develop a natural rapport with your listeners.

If you forget what comes next or get stuck in a story, ask the youngsters to repeat what's happened thus far (giving you time to think) or suggest what could come next.

After hearing a few stories, children will begin to try to figure out the object you are drawing before you fold it together. Then, when you fold the drawing together and they find out they have guessed correctly—what a thrill!

You will know by a child's facial expression when he or she knows what it is that you are drawing. If you notice a listener just bursting to "spill" the answer, recognize him or her quietly with an aside such as, "Shhh . . . it's a secret!"

4. When you are storytelling to a large group, you will want to tape the drawing paper to a wall or chalkboard. You could even enlarge the picture with an opaque projector to make it more easily seen. Drawing on lined chart or plain chart paper also works well. Use the lines to help you keep the two halves lined up properly. If you have just a few listeners, everyone could sit around a table.

5. Retell the story at least once. Retelling the story gives the listener a second chance to enjoy it as well as to learn the story and the drawing steps. Stories can and should be changed by each storyteller, and a story will be a little different each time it is told.

Mystery-Fold variations

1. **Fold Together**—The simplest Mystery-Fold story is told while drawing on both the left and right sides of the paper and then folding the sides together at the end of the story to make the picture. Depending on the picture you are drawing, the paper can be held horizontally or vertically. You can draw the picture sideways or upside down if you feel the picture will be easily guessed. At the end of the story, fold the paper together and turn it right side up.

2. **Single Fold**—A way to vary the Mystery-Fold story is to fold over a section of the lower or upper part of the paper to partially cover up a section of your drawing. You then can draw on this new part of the paper, relating it to your story and picture. For example, you draw a flower complete with roots. Fold up the lower section of paper to cover up the roots and draw a flowerpot on it.

3. **Double Fold**—Folding the edges of the paper to meet in the middle and make "doors" is a fun way to tell a story. Open the doors at the end of the story to reveal a second drawing (previously made). Or—fold the "doors" to only partially cover your drawing. Folded like this, the picture becomes something else, and you can draw on the closed "doors" to change your picture into a new one.

4. **Other Folds**—You don't have to fold the paper at all. If you see an object that looks like one thing, but when turned upside down or sideways looks like something else, use that idea for a story! (See "The Unhappy Office Building.") You also can tell a story that involves two folds or

precut flaps that fold up or down to cover or uncover parts of your drawing.

There are countless variations of drawing and folding. You and your students will surprise yourselves at how creative you can be with the Mystery-Fold concept.

How to teach Mystery-Fold stories

Mystery-Fold stories are easy to teach, but concentrate on just one type at a time.

1. Start with the basic fold, presented in "Fold Together," the first section in this book. Tell several stories from this chapter. Then retell one story several times so that you and the listeners can tell the story together.

2. After you have told the story once or twice together, distribute paper *only* to each child. Explain the folding directions first. The paper should be folded in half, then the right side folded back on itself. Let everyone practice folding and unfolding their papers.

3. Now you are ready to hand out pencils. Encourage the children to look around the room and pick out an object that seems easy to draw. They should think about where to divide the drawing and then sketch it on their *folded* paper.

4. Encourage each listener to come up with his or her own story using the basic Mystery-Fold. It is easiest to make the drawing first, and then think up a story to go with it.

5. This is a great time to teach story elements. Every story needs the following:

   A   an introduction
   B.   characters
   C.   location or setting
   D.   action or plot
   E.   resolution or good ending

6. Expect very simple, imperfect drawings and stories from your listeners at first. Their stories might even be remarkably similar to one that you have just told. That is okay—and quite a compliment to you!

You might need to encourage a reluctant child who "just can't think of anything." Help him draw a picture from one printed on his shirt, or start her off with a piece of jewelry that she is wearing. (The "Skateboarding" story in this book comes from just such a starting point; it came from a necklace that a student had on that day.) Get the child started with questions such as, "What else does a skateboard look like? Where should you divide the drawing?"

7. Plan to have several sheets of paper for each student. Encourage them to practice telling their story to themselves first and then to a friend. When they tell it to you, you can help them "work out the bugs ."

8. After several practices with small groups of friends, your storytellers will be ready to present to the rest of the class. After their presentation, you might want to reward each child with a "Storytelling Certificate" or another story told by you.

How to create your own Mystery-Fold stories

1. Decide on a story to tell, then choose something to draw and fold that is an integral part of the story. Or choose an object to draw, then find a story or write a story involving that object. "How to draw" books (available in most libraries) are great resource for ideas.

2. A basic Mystery-Fold is done by folding the paper in half across the width of the paper, then folding it in half again. Make this fold parallel to the first, which will divide that paper equally into four long

rectangular sections. Return to the first fold, and fold the end rectangular section back onto the adjacent one. Now only the two end sections are visible; the middle two sections are not.

3. Prefold your paper and draw lines lightly with a pencil. During the telling of your story, relate the drawing steps to the storyline. For example, as a character goes places or does things, add new lines to the picture.

4. Drawings do not have to be symmetrical. You can take any simple drawing, divide it in half, and draw one half on one side of the page and the other half on the other side. Drawings may be divided in half horizontally or vertically, depending on what is being depicted.

   Remember, the picture is drawn on the end sections only. If you feel the picture will be easily guessed while you are telling the story, draw your picture upside down or sideways.

5. If you are drawing a picture that is symmetrical, the second character can repeat what the first character said. For example, Mom can ask, "Did you look under the laundry?" (draw one half of the bear's body) and Tom can reply, "Yes, I did" (draw the other half of the bear's body).

   Asking and answering question is a great way to tell a story. Both the story-lines and the drawing lines are repeated and symmetrical. This makes it easy for a child to remember.

6. Using your imagination, you can come up with all kinds of stories and ways to Mystery-Fold! A few simple tips will guarantee a pleasurable, successful story session every time.

To guarantee your success

1. Select an appropriate story for your listeners.

2. Trace lightly over all drawing lines on your paper.

3. Draw in any lines with a marker if required for your story.

4. Prefold on all fold lines.

5. Use masking tape to mount the drawing paper on a chalkboard, easel, or other hard surface.

6. Be familiar with the story.

7. Be ready (with additional sheets of prepared paper) to tell the Mystery-Fold story several times. You will hear, "Tell it again!"

8. Have in mind some ideas for discussion after you tell the story.

9. Have paper and pencils ready for your listeners if you plan on asking them to participate.

10. Enjoy yourself!

Fold Together

Grandma's House

Prefold paper and tape to a hard surface.

Optional introductory statement: "By the time we get to the end of this story, you will recognize it as a story you already know."

Once there was a grandson who just loved to visit his grandma's. Lots of kids go to their grandma's house, but this house was special. Let me describe it to you.

It had a tower on each side. *(**Draw from 1 to 2 to 3 to 4 to 5, then from 6 to 7 to 8 to 9 to 10. Draw from A to B to C, then from D to E to F. These are the towers and inside roof line.**)*

The roof was curved, and the grandson thought it looked like a sunrise. *(**Draw from 4 to 7.**)*

This house had lots of windows, and the grandson liked to go from window to window, looking out of them. *(**Draw six long rectangle windows: G, H, I, J, K, and L.**)*

Sometimes he'd stop for a while at a window. He liked to look out at the wide front lawn and imagine all kinds of things. He pretended that the grass was really water. The lawn had big stepping stones all the way across it. This made a great bridge across the water. *(**Draw six wide rectangles across the bottom: M, N, O P, Q, and R.**)*

At one window he would look out and imagine a small mountain goat leaping across the bridge. *(**Draw a line in window G.**)* This is the goat jumping over the bridge. *(**Draw a zigzag in box M.**)*

At another window he would look out and see two mountain goats traipsing across the bridge. *(**Draw a line in window L.**)* They were bigger than the first goat.

These are the goats running across the bridge. *(**Draw zigzags in boxes Q and R.**)* They were trying to get away from something—something that was under the bridge.

Do you know what the boy saw next? He saw the biggest billy goat turn back . . . back to get the . . . TROLL! *(**Untape and fold paper together quickly to show the troll.**)*

Optional Activities

1. Discuss how the house is folded into a troll.
2. Get a copy of *The Three Billy Goats Gruff* and read or tell the story.
3. What other stories do you know that have the number three in them? (*The Three Bears, Magic Fish, The Three Sillies,* etc.)

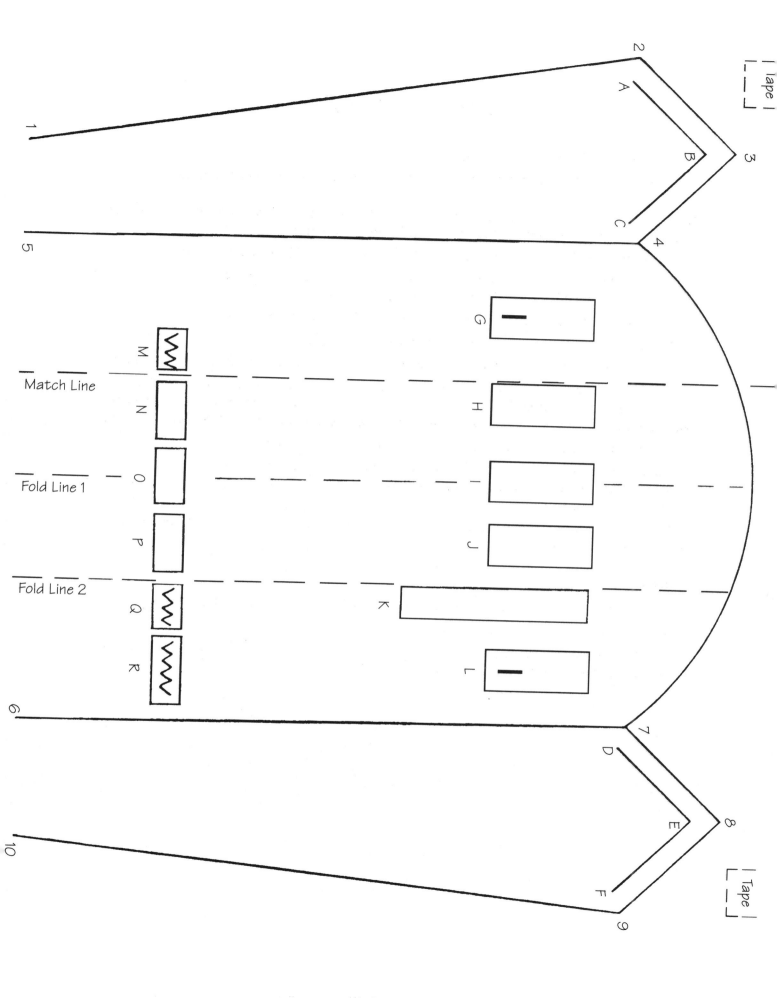

The Birthday Party

Prefold paper and tape to a hard surface.

Optional introductory statement: "Here is an unusual story about a birthday party."

Jessica lived on an island in the middle of a lake. (***Draw a large circle and small circle within it on the right side of the paper. This is the duck's head and eye.***)

It was her birthday, and her mom said she could have five friends over for a birthday party.

Even though she lived on an island, she had lots of friends. Jessica said, "I think I'll ask my friend, the porcupine." (***Draw the rabbit's nose and whiskers.***)

"I think I should ask the twins, the caterpillars." (***Draw the rabbit's ears.***)

Jessica also asked her friend, the fly. (***Draw the rabbit's mouth.***)

And even her ladybug friend could come to the party! (***Draw the rabbit's head and eyes.***)

"Let's see, I have invited the porcupine, the twin caterpillars, the fly, and the ladybug to my party. (***Point to each animal as you say it.***) Who else shall I ask?" (***Pause and let the listeners tell you that you have just drawn a rabbit. Untape the paper and rotate it to show the rabbit.***)

When Jessica asked the rabbit to her party, that made six friends.

But Jessica was worried. She said, "How will all my friends get to my house in the middle of the lake? (***Indicate house again as you are holding the paper.***) Oh, I know! I'll just give them a ride from the shore to my island!"

Do you know what animal Jessica is? (***Fold the paper together and rotate to show the duck.***) That's right! Jessica is a . . . DUCK!

Optional Activities

1. An island is an unusual place to hold a party. Where would you like to have a party?

2. What other animals could help the friends get across the water?

3. Classify the animals listed in the story into the categories of mammal, insect, bird, etc. What are the defining characteristics of each category?

Tape

Match Line

Fold Line 1

Fold Line 2

Tape

The Favorite Animal

Prefold paper. Have both an orange and a black marker ready. Tape picture sideways to a hard surface when indicated in the story.

Optional introductory statement: "Have you ever been to a zoo? (Pause.) What is your favorite animal?"

One day Mr. Tyler said, "Class, tomorrow we are going to the zoo. I want you all to draw one animal that you hope to see there, then we'll talk about it."

Lindsay got out her markers, but she had trouble thinking of anything. Soon it was her turn to show her animal to the rest of the class. She walked up to the front of the room. Her paper was blank. *(Indicate the blank paper in your hand.)*

"I couldn't think of any certain animal. I like them all," said Lindsay.

"Well, we'll help you," said Mr. Tyler. "Tape your paper up there and draw what I draw on your side of the paper." *(Tape the paper to the chalkboard. Show Lindsay's side of the paper by pointing to the right side of paper.)*

"Do you like sharks?" asked Mr. Tyler. He drew a shark fin on his side. *(Draw line 1 with the orange marker. This is the tiger's left ear.)*

Lindsay answered, "No, I don't. They are too scary." *(Draw line 2. This is the tiger's right ear.)*

"Do you like big black bugs?" asked Mr. Tyler. *(Draw and color in at 3. This is the tiger's eye.)*

"No! Bugs! Yuck!" Lindsay drew a bug just like the teacher's. *(Draw and color in at 4. This is the tiger's other eye.)*

"Do you like bats that hang upside down in caves?" Mr. Tyler drew a cave with a bat in it. *(Draw a half circle at 5 and a solid triangle for 6. This is half of the tiger's nose.)*

"No! Does the zoo really have bats to look at?" Lindsay drew her cave and bat. *(Draw a half circle at 7 and a triangle for 8. This is the other half of the tiger's nose.)*

"Is your favorite animal a fish that you can catch with a hook?" Mr. Tyler drew just a hook. *(Draw 9. This is half of the tiger's mouth.)*

"Don't be silly. You can't go fishing in a zoo." Lindsay drew a hook, too. *(Draw 10. This is the other half of the tiger's mouth.)*

"Then it must be an iguana. One of those with long, sharp tails." Mr. Tyler drew the iguana's tail with his black marker. *(Draw a zigzag for line 11 with the black marker. These are the tiger's stripes.)*

"No, it's not an iguana." Lindsay used her black marker also. *(Draw a zigzag for line 12. These are also the tiger's stripes.)*

"These are all my guesses. I give up! What is your favorite animal?" asked Mr. Tyler as he drew a big circle around his guesses. *(Using the orange marker, draw line 13. This is half of the tiger's face.)*

"Okay," said Lindsay as she drew her last line. *(Draw line 14. This is the other half of the tiger's face.)* "Want me to tell you what it is?" *(Untape paper, fold, and turn right side up.)*

"It's a . . . TIGER!"

Optional Activities

1. Draw your favorite animal. What does it eat? Where does it live?

2. Did you know that tigers like to swim? That is unusual for a member of the cat family. What other facts can we find out about tigers?

3. There are several animals mentioned in this story. Read and discuss more about them.

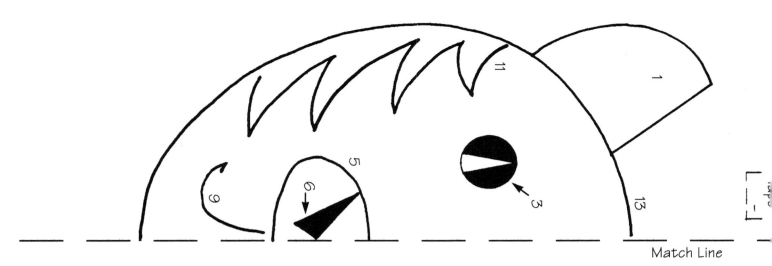

Match Line

Fold Line 1

Fold Line 2

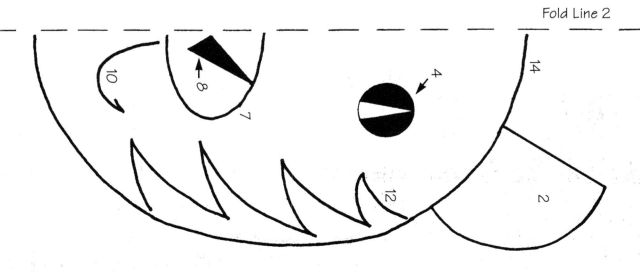

Renee's Pet

Prefold paper and tape to a hard surface.

Optional introductory statement: "Have you ever had a pet? Here's a story about one."

One day at school Renee said to her best friend Marie, "Hey, I got a new pet for my birthday! Can you guess what it is?"

"Is it a snail with a round back and a big eye?" Marie drew a snail on her paper. ***(Draw a half circle and a small circle within it on the left side of the paper, line 1.)***

"No. It's not a snail with a round back." Renee reached across to Marie's desk and also drew a snail and eye on the other side. ***(Draw another half circle and smaller circle within it on the right side of the page, line 2.)***

"Is it a fish with a big fin on its back?" Marie drew a fish with a fin. ***(Draw the larger half circle with the triangular attachment on the left side of the paper, lines 3 and 4.)***

"No, it's not a fish with a big fin on its back." Renee drew a fish with a big fin on her side of the paper. ***(Draw the larger half circle with the triangular attachment on the right side of the paper, lines 5 and 6.)***

"Is it a smaller fish, maybe a minnow?" Marie drew a small minnow on her side of the paper. ***(Draw the pair of curves on the left side of the paper, line 7.)***

"No, it's not a minnow," laughed Renee, and she drew a minnow, too. ***(Draw the pair of curves on the right side of the paper, line 8.)***

"Okay, you get only one more guess," said Renee.

Marie drew a big black spot. ***(Draw a circle with a spot in it on the left side of the paper, line 9.)*** "Is it a big black bug?"

"No, it's not a big black bug." Renee drew a black spot on her side of the paper. ***(Draw a circle with a spot in it on the right side of the paper, line 10)*** "I'll just have to tell you." ***(Untape paper and fold it together.)***

"It's a . . . PIG!"

Optional Activities

1. Tell a story about an unusual pet you had once or wished you had.

2. Would you like to have a pig for a pet? What are the advantages and disadvantages of a pet pig?

3. There are lots of stories about pigs. Could you find one in the library?

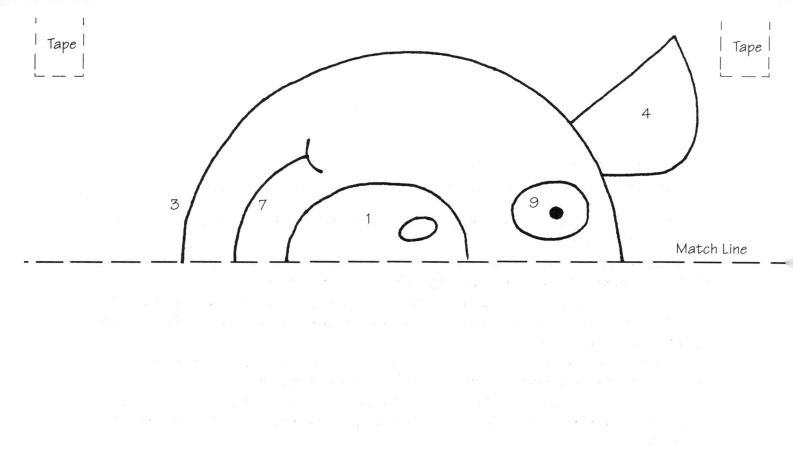

Match Line

Fold Line 1

Fold Line 2

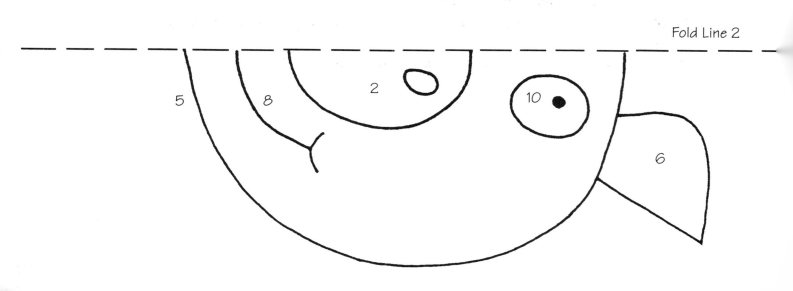

A Drink for a Crow

Prefold paper and tape to a hard surface.

Optional introductory statement: "This is a story that people have told for many years. It's one that you really have to think about."

Once there was a crow who was very thirsty. He remembered seeing a jar the day before that contained some cool, clear water. So, he flew into the sky in search of the jar. ***(Draw from 1 to 2.)***

After several long, hot hours, the crow spotted the jar. He dove down and landed on the rim. ***(Draw from 3 to 4.)*** But when he tried to drink, he found that he could not reach down far enough into the jar with his beak. ***(Draw from 5 to 6.)***

No matter how hard he tried to reach, he just could not quite get to the water! ***(Draw from 7 to 8.)***

The crow was just about to give up when he got an idea. He flew to a nearby road and picked up something small and hard in his beak. ***(Draw a circle in the top right section, 9.)***

He then flew back and dropped it into the jar. ***(Draw a circle in the bottom left section of the jar, 10.)***

The crow did this again. He flew to the road and picked up something small in his beak. ***(Draw another circle in the top right section of the jar, 11.)*** He then returned and dropped it into the jar. ***(Draw another circle in the bottom left section of the jar, 12.)***

The crow did this again and again. ***(Draw more circles in the top and bottom sections.)***

At last he could drink easily from the jar. ***(Untape paper and fold together.)***

Do you know what the crow filled the jar up with?

Yes! That's right, small ROCKS.

Why did the crow fill the jar with rocks? What did the rocks do to the water level in the jar?

Yes, the rocks made the WATER RISE to the top of the jar. That was a pretty smart crow, don't you think?

Optional Activities

1. Read and discuss other Aesop's fables.

2. Make up your own Aesop's fable and share it with the class.

3. Do you think a crow could really figure out this problem?

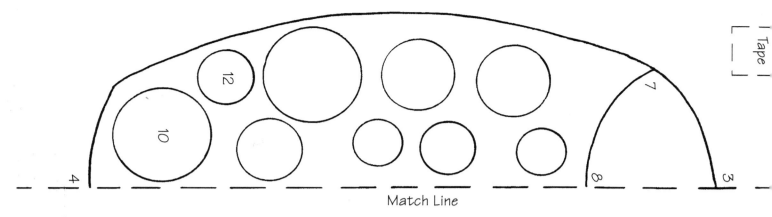

Match Line

Fold Line 1

Fold Line 2

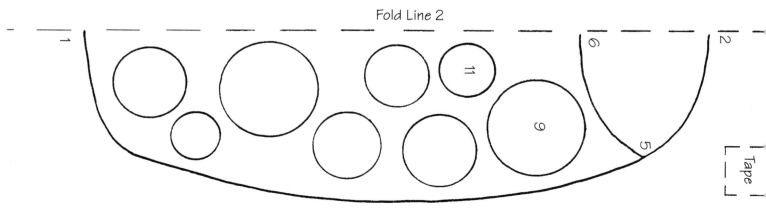

Matt's Missing Toy

Prefold paper and tape to a hard surface.

Optional introductory statement: "Have you ever lost anything? This is a story about someone who lost his favorite toy."

"I can't find it," said Matt.

"Did you look under the table?" asked his mom. ***(Draw from 1 to 2 to 3. This is half of the bear's body and head.)***

"Yes, no luck," Matt replied. ***(Draw from 4 to 5 to 6. This is the other half of the bear's body and head.)***

"Well, then how about under the laundry?" suggested his mom. ***(Draw line 7. This is the bear's left paw.)***

"I looked there, too. Where do you think it is?" Matt was worried now. ***(Draw line 8. This is the bear's right paw.)***

"I bet it's in the yard," said his mom. "Why don't you go look around there?" ***(Draw line 9. This is the bear's left ear.)***

"Good idea!" Matt looked all around his yard but couldn't find it anywhere. ***(Draw line 10. This is the bear's right ear.)***

"I think I'll go ask Patrick. Maybe he has it." Matt pulled the door open. ***(Draw 11. This is the bear's left eye.)*** He walked down the street to his friend's house. ***(Draw line 12. This is the bear's left leg.)*** Matt walked home again. ***(Draw line 13. This is the bear's right leg.)***

When he got home he shut the door ***(Draw 14, bear's right eye.)*** and said, "I walked down to Patrick's house and back. I just can't find it anywhere."

Matt sat down. He sat on something! "Wait a minute, here it is!" ***(Untape and fold the paper together, then turn it right side up.)***

Matt smiled, "I found it." ***(Draw a smile across the folded paper.)***

Do you know what Matt was looking for? Yes, it was his . . . TEDDY BEAR!

Optional Activities

1. Tell a story about a time when you lost your favorite toy. Where did you find it?

2. Have you ever found anything that someone else lost? What did you do with it?

3. What would be the worst thing you can think of to lose?

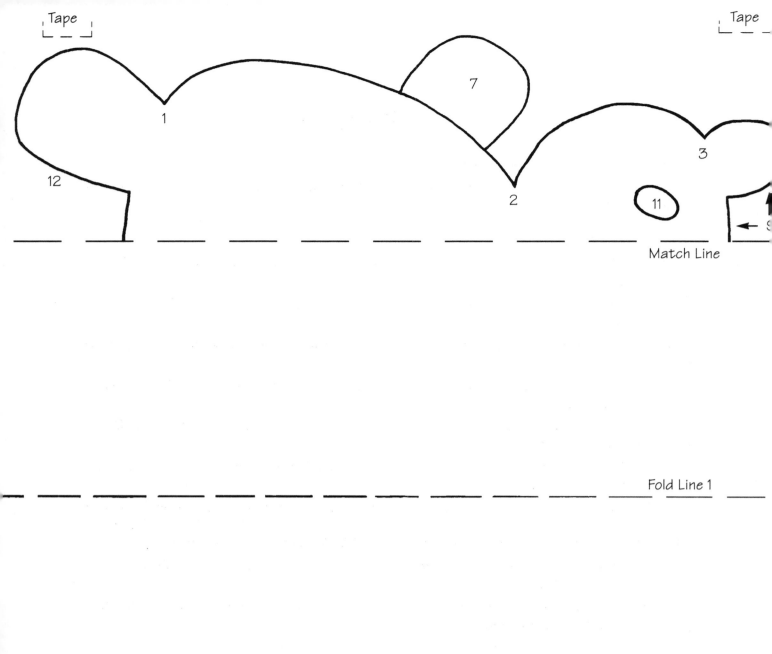

Match Line

Fold Line 1

Fold Line 2

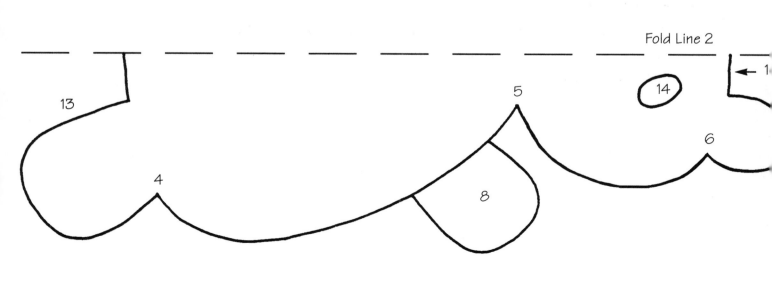

Single Fold

Lily

Prefold paper and tape to a hard surface.

Optional introductory statement: "Storms can sometimes do lots of damage. Here's a story about one."

The other night there was a storm. When Lily woke up in the morning, she found herself on the ground in a mess. She needed a comb. *(**Draw lines 1 through 6. These are the roots.**)*

Her arms were all droopy. *(**Draw two straight lines, 7 and 8. This is the body. Then draw lines 9 and 10. These are the arms.**)*

Even her clothes needed straightening. *(**Draw 11. This is the petal.**)*

"I need someone to come along and help me fix myself up. I feel all upside down," she said.

Just then someone did come along. Lily was picked up, turned around, and straightened up. *(**Untape paper and turn it over to show the flower.**)*

She was put in a very safe place. *(**Fold the bottom of the paper up and draw the flowerpot, line 12, on the front fold.**)*

Do you know what Lily is? Yes, Lily is a . . . FLOWER . . . in a . . . FLOWERPOT!

Optional Activities

1. Name other flowers that are also girls' names (Rose, Daisy, Violet, etc.).
2. Discuss plants and what they need in order to live.
3. Tell a story about a flower who turned into a girl, or vice versa.

To make the Lily: *Use one sheet of paper, drawing the flower pattern on one side and the flower pot on the other. Fold paper up to complete the match. Draw patterns with top and bottom matches as shown.*

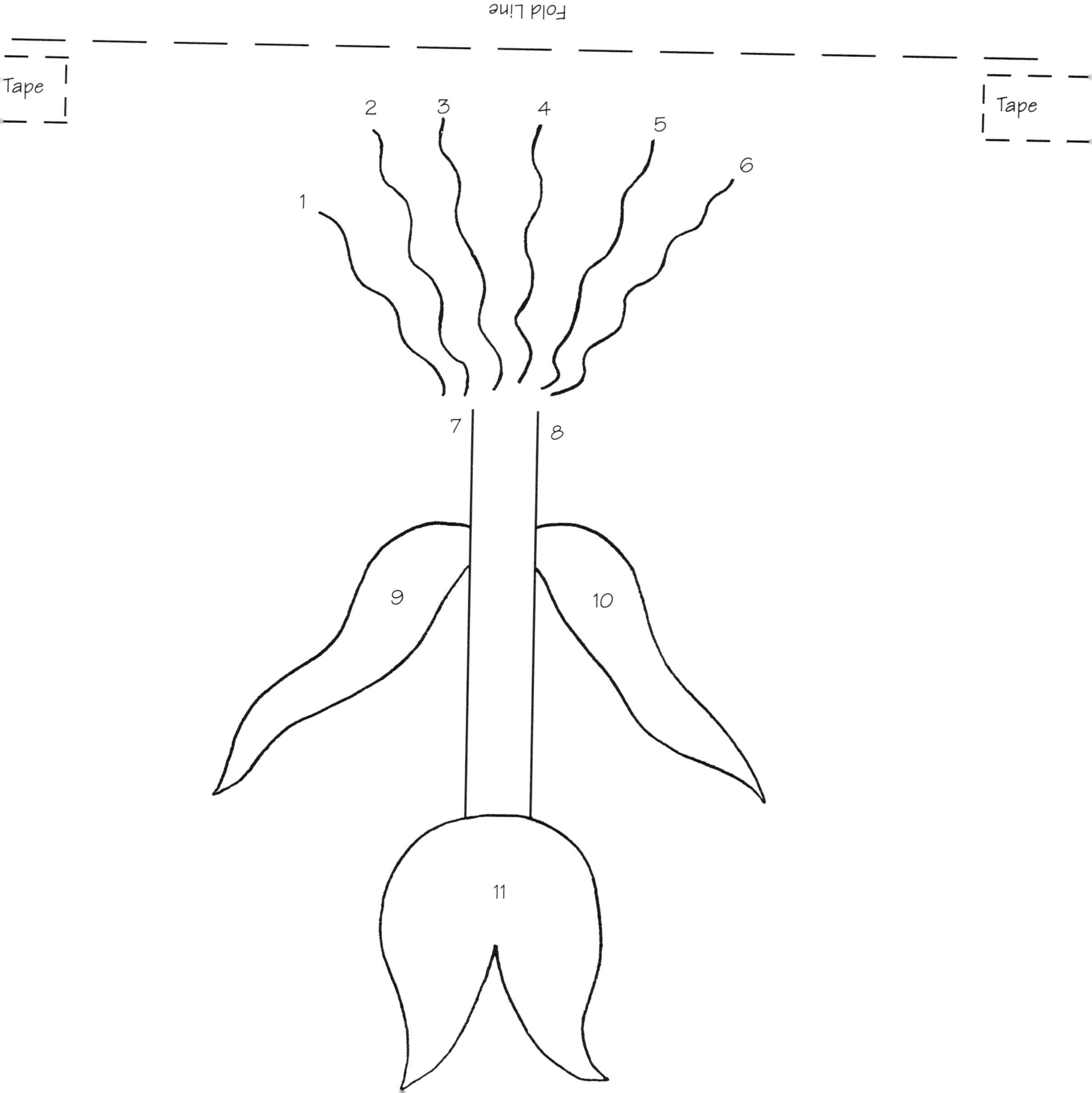

Fold Line

Fold Line

Tape

Tape

1

2   3   4

5

6

7   8

9   10

11

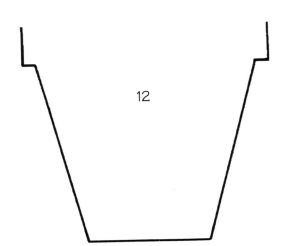

12

Soccer

Prefold paper and tape to a hard surface. Use a brown marker on white paper.

Optional introductory statement: "What sports do you like to play? Here's a story about a really fun sport called soccer."

Once there were two friends, Scott and Megan, who loved to play soccer. ***(Draw the large circle, line 1. This is the soccer ball.)***

One day after winning a big game, the two were really hungry. They tried to think of what they wanted to eat. "How about some crackers?" suggested Scott. ***(Draw and color in three pentagons, lines 2, 3, and 4. These are the soccer spots.)***

"No, let's get some hamburgers," said Megan. ***(Draw and color in three more pentagons, lines 5, 6, and 7.)***

"I have it! How about some cookies?" said Scott. ***(Draw and color in two more pentagons, lines 8 and 9. At this point, your listeners will figure out that you have just drawn a soccer ball and will mention this to you.)***

Megan and Scott could not agree on what to eat, so Megan said, "I have a plan. You go that way, Scott." ***(Draw short line 10.)*** "And I'll go this way." ***(Draw short line 11.)*** "We'll both get something to eat and I'll see you tomorrow at practice."

Scott said, "Okay. Bye."

(Fold up the bottom of the paper.) The two friends both left and walked until they came to a place where they really wanted to get a snack! ***(Extend lines 10 and 11 to meet at point 12.)***

Can you believe that they ended up in the same store? Guess what they both had to eat? Yes, an . . . ICE CREAM CONE!

What flavor do you think it could be? Right . . . a CHOCOLATE CHIP ICE CREAM CONE! ***(Accept other answers also.)***

Optional Activities

1. The ice cream cone makes a person think of a piece of pizza. How could we change this story to include pizza? Perhaps Scott and Megan first decide to eat a slice of pizza and then go for ice cream?

2. Discuss some healthy food choices for a snack. (This could lead to a conversation about the basic food groups.)

3. Is there a particular food that makes you think of something else, too, that you could develop a story around?

> **To make Ice Cream Cone:** *Use one sheet of paper, drawing the soccer ball on one side and the base of the cone on the other. Fold paper up to complete the match. Draw patterns with top and bottom matches as shown.*

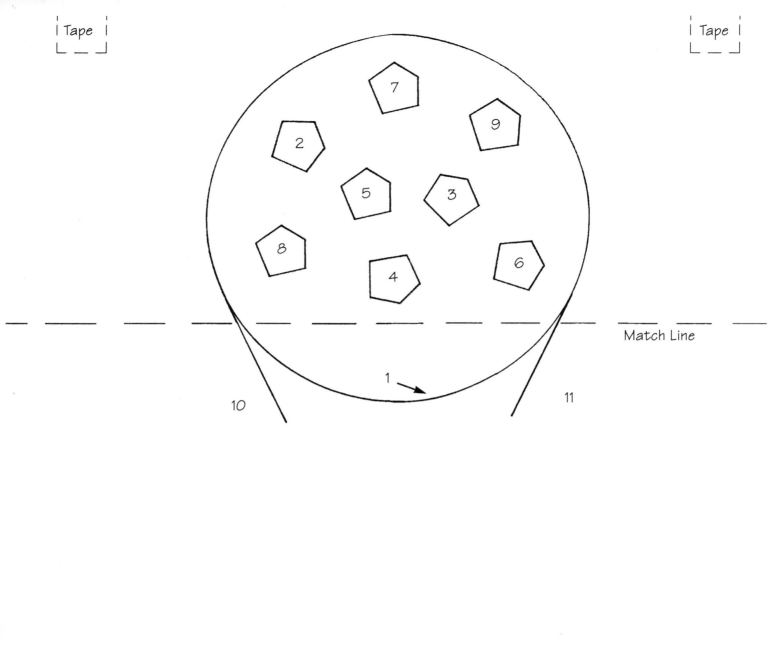

Match Line

Fold Line 1

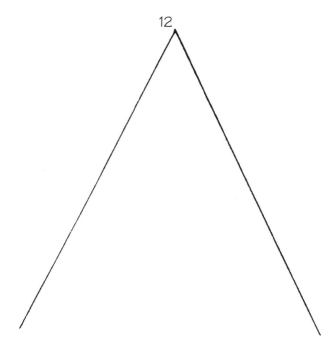

Shut De Door

Tell this in a hushed, confidential, spooky voice. Fold paper in half before beginning the story, and draw the monster on the back before taping to a hard surface. Be careful not to let the audience see it.

Optional introductory statement: "Everyone's heard of the Bogeyman. He's a pretend monster that looks exactly like you want him to look. This is a story about him."

If you live way back in the thick part of the woods, you know not to go out on hot, dark nights when it's pitch black outside. You light your candle but keep all your doors and windows shut tight. Because that's when the Bogeyman likes to come out of his cave. His cave is hidden deep in the woods. (*Draw from 1 to 2 to 3 on the right side of the page. This is the candle flame.*)

When he comes out of his cave, he walks straight along looking for a light. (*Draw from 1 to 4. This is the left side of the candle.*)

When the Bogeyman sees someone with a candle, he grabs 'em! (*Draw the oval from 4 to 5 quickly and definitely. This is the candle base.*)

And he takes 'em back to his cave! (*Draw from 5 to 3. This is the right side of the candle. Pause.*)

There's only one thing to do on those hot, dark nights so you don't get caught by that ol' Bogeyman! Light your candle (*indicate drawing*), but shut your door up tight. (*Fold left side of paper over the right with a loud slam and draw circle 6. This is the doorknob. Quickly draw lines 7 and 8 across the top then 9 and 10 across the bottom. This makes it look more like a door.*)

If you get even one or two or three holes in your door (*Draw small triangles 11, 12 and 13 for claws.*), the Bogeyman will see your light through the holes, and he will come after you. (*Quickly turn paper over to show the monster that you have previously drawn.*)

So . . . shut de door, and keep the Bogeyman in the night!

Optional Activities

1. Do you know any other scary stories?

2. Draw a monster or some other scary picture to share with the class. Make up a story to go with it.

3. Discuss the difference between real and make-believe. What kind of story is this?

To make Shut De Door: *Use one sheet of paper, drawing the candle on one side and the monster on the other. Fold paper over to complete the match. Draw patterns with top and bottom matches as shown.*

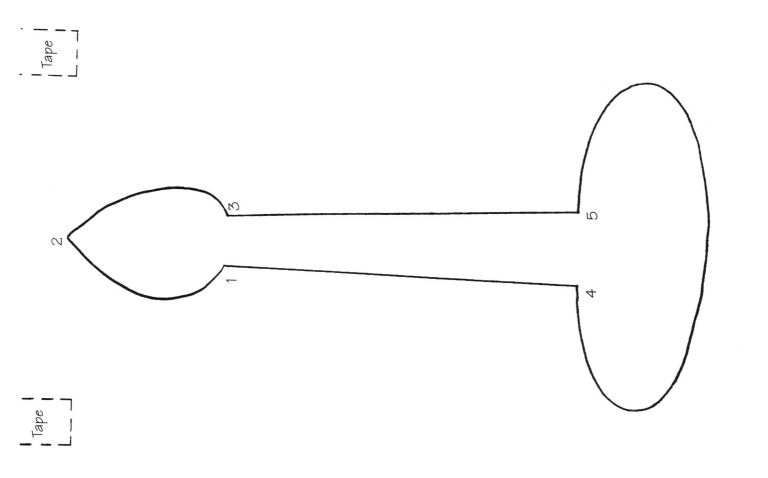

Tape

Tape

2

3

1

5

4

Fold Line

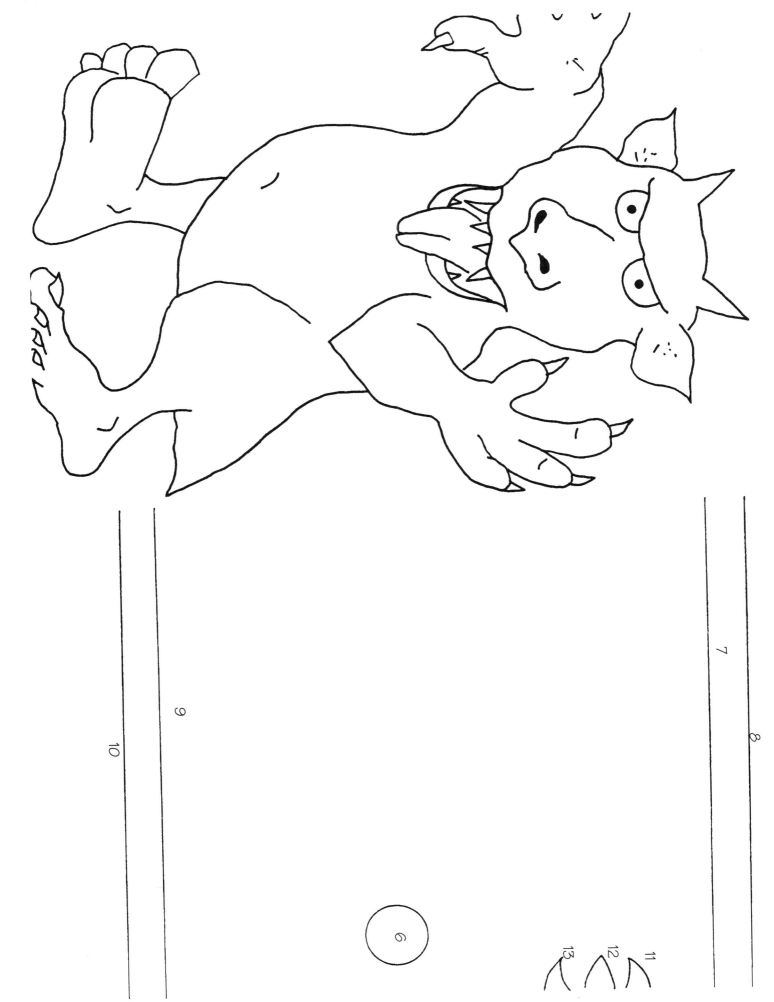

Skateboarding

Prefold paper and tape to a hard surface.

Optional introductory statement: "Have you ever ridden on a skateboard? This is a story about a kid who had one."

Jeremy loved to skateboard. Every day he would skateboard all the way around his block. ***(Draw from 1 to 2 to 3, then connect back to 1. Draw two small circles for wheels, 4 and 5.)***

One day while he was skateboarding, he saw a dark shadow on the ground. He looked up in the sky and saw something big, but it wasn't an airplane. "What could it be?" he wondered.

The next day, as he was skateboarding around his block, Jeremy saw the big thing in the sky again. ***(Fold paper up from the bottom and draw from 6 to 7.)***

It did cast a huge shadow on the ground. ***(Draw from 8 to 9.)***

The shadow even covered up several houses. ***(Draw squares 10 to 14.)*** Do you know what Jeremy saw while he was skateboarding? (Open picture up to show skateboard again.)

Yes, it was a BLIMP! ***(Fold picture back up to show how the two pictures relate. Discuss how the houses become the windows on the blimp, and the shadow is the passenger cab of the blimp.)***

Optional Activities

1. Find out more about blimps and how they are used.

2. What kind of shadows do other vehicles that travel in the air cast?

3. Learn more about shadows: what causes them, and how they change during the course of the day.

To make the Blimp: *Use one sheet of paper, drawing the skateboard on one side and the base of the blimp on the other. Fold paper up to complete the match. Draw patterns with top and bottom matches as shown.*

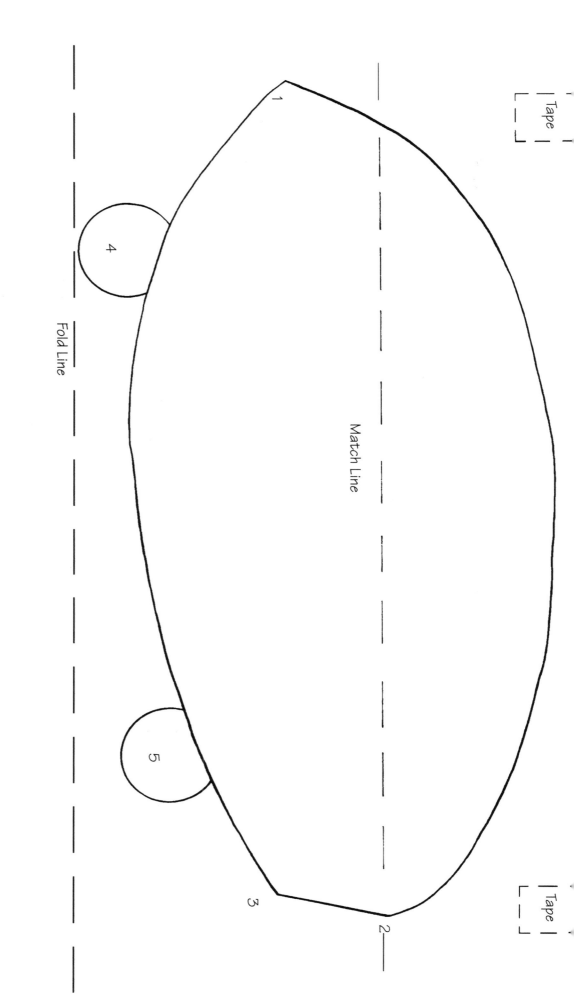

Tape

Tape

Fold Line

Match Line

1

2

3

4

5

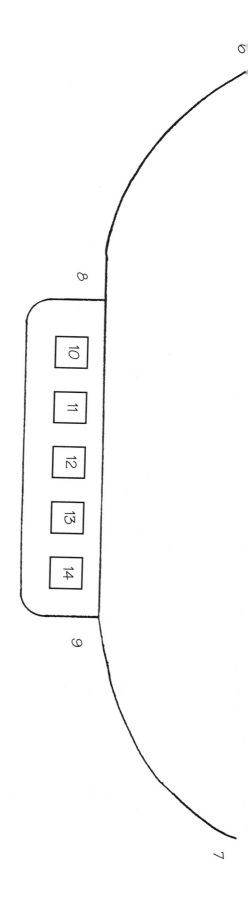

What Jessica and Rachel Had

Prefold paper and tape to a hard surface.

Optional introductory statement: *"This is a story about two girls who lived an unusual life."*

Rachel and Jessica were sisters who had everything they needed. Well, almost everything. If you were to look in the windows of their house, here are the rooms that you would see.

Through one window, you would see the living room. *(**Draw square 1.**)*

In the next window, you would see their bedroom. *(**Draw square 2.**)*

The kitchen was the next room. *(**Draw square 3.**)*

Jessica and Rachel had their own toy room *(**Draw square 4.**)* and, of course, a bathroom. *(**Draw square 5.**)*

Why, you would even see a special schoolroom set up for the girls if you looked in the next window. *(**Draw square 6.**)*

Jessica and Rachel were very well traveled. They had made trips to several faraway islands. *(**Draw a circle above each square.**)*

The girls had been all the way around the world twice! The first time the trip took a year. *(**Draw from 7 to 8 to 9 to 10 then back to 7.**)* The second time they went slower, and so it took longer. *(**Draw from 10 to 11 to 12 to 13 to 14, then back to 10.**)*

The reason that Jessica and Rachel traveled so much was because of their dad's job. What do you think he was in charge of? *(**Pause and let listeners supply the answer.**)* Yes! That's right! A SHIP! He was captain of a big ship!

This ship had big chimneys where the smoke came out. *(**Draw rectangles A, B, and C, including crossbars at the top of each.**)* And it had two big radio antennas. *(**Draw lines 15, 16, 17, and 18.**)* That's how Jessica and Rachel talked to their teacher while they were at sea—by two-way radio. The teacher taught them their lessons over the radio!

Jessica and Rachel were very happy. As I said, they had almost everything that kids who live on land have. *(**Untape paper. Fold up the page from the bottom, and turn the illustration over.**)*

Do you know what they didn't have? That's right . . . a SWING SET!

Optional Activities

1. What do you think life on board a ship would be like? What are some things you would like about it? not like about it?

2. Children live very different lives in different parts of the world. This would be an interesting topic to research.

3. There are lots of different types of ships. Perhaps you could find out more about them in the library.

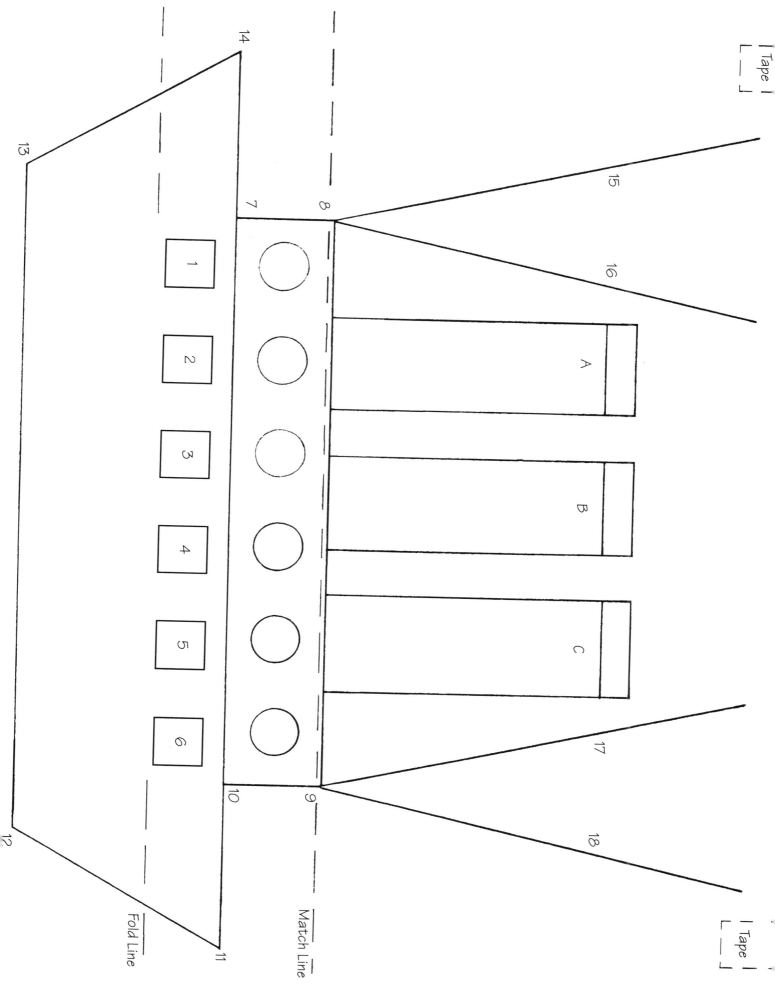

Zoo Rides

Tell this story with the paper folded together and taped to a hard surface. Draw the top of the notes with the connecting note bar before telling the story.

Optional introductory statement: "Have you ever been to the zoo? Or ridden on an animal?"

Once there was a special animal ride at the Children's Zoo. All the kids loved to ride this animal, and the first thing they would do when they arrived at the zoo was race down the winding path to the animal rides. (***Draw from 1 to 2. This is the camel's front, face, and ears.***)

Then they would stand in line for what seemed a really long time. (***Draw from 2 to 3. This is the back of the camel's neck.***)

At last they each got to ride him around and around. (***Draw from 3 to 4. These are the camel's humps.***)

When the ride was over, the kids would jump off and run all the way around to stand in line again. (***Draw from 4 back to 1. This forms the camel's tail and lower body and retraces the head.***)

It was great fun for them, but not so much fun for the . . . (***pause to let listeners name the animal.***) That's right, CAMEL. He got so tired. His legs ached (***draw all four legs***) and his feet got all swollen. (***Draw feet, 5, 6, 7, and 8.***)

Some days he was so tired that he walked really slowly, and no one could make him hurry. Then the camel ride wasn't much fun. But one day the zookeeper discovered something that made the camel much happier and peppier. As long as the zookeeper did this certain thing, the camel had no trouble giving the children rides, even if there were quite a few children in line. Do you know what made this camel happy? (***Lift the top of page to reveal the musical notes.***)

Yes, it was MUSIC. The zookeeper played his radio for the children's camel, and he loved it!

Optional Activities

1. Talk about musical notes and what they mean.
2. Make a list of all the animals that it would be possible to ride on.
3. What makes you feel better when you get tired? Discuss some "pick-me-ups."

> **To make the Camel:** *Use one sheet of paper, drawing the camel's body on one side and the musical notes on the other. Fold paper over musical notes and lift to reveal them. Draw patterns with top and bottom matches as shown.*

Fold Line

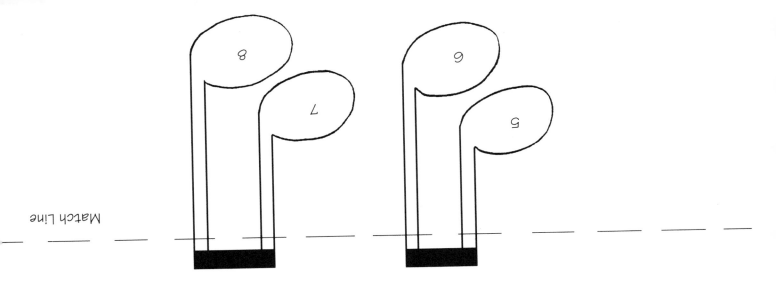

Tape

Fold Line

Tape

The Racetrack

Start this story with the paper folded and taped to a hard surface.

Optional introductory statement: "This is a story about a boy with a great birthday tradition."

Ryan's favorite thing to do was to go to the racetrack. Every spring, on his birthday, Ryan's mom would take him there to see the whizzing cars.

This racetrack was unusual because it was in the shape of an . . . *(Draw an "eight" on the paper, line 1, then pause and let listeners identify it.).* That's right, it's a FIGURE 8.

Sometimes Ryan and his mom Anne would sit up high to watch the cars. *(Draw top inside circle, line 2.)* And sometimes they would sit down low. *(Draw bottom inside circle, line 3.)*

On one birthday at the track, Ryan's mom said to him, "Ryan, today you are as old as the shape of this track."

Ryan answered, "Yes, the track and I are both eight. But how long have we been coming here on my birthday?"

His mom thought for a minute and said, "Since you were . . ." *(Open out paper and quickly draw end lines 4, 5, and 6 to complete the numeral "three.").*

Yes, Ryan has been to the racetrack every year since he was THREE!

Optional Activities

1. What are some things that you like to do on your birthday?
2. Does your family have any traditions that you celebrate?
3. Find out more about race car drivers, their cars, and their careers.

To make the Racetrack: *Use one sheet of paper, drawing the number three on one side and the other half of the eight on the other. Fold paper over to make the eight. Draw patterns with top and bottom matches as shown.*

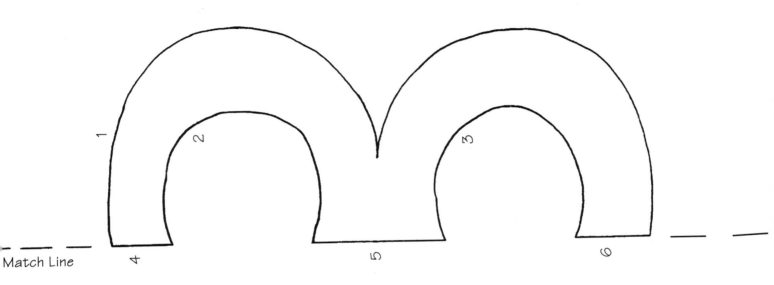

Match Line

1 2 3

4 5 6

Tape

Fold Line

Double Fold

A Halloween Scare

Draw a ghost on the middle third of the paper. Fold both sides of the paper together to meet in the middle. These form the doors over the ghost. Tape the paper to a hard surface on both sides of the ghost, then close the doors and tape these together with a third piece of tape. Your audience should not see the ghost.

Optional introductory statement: "Have you ever been scared on Halloween night? Here's a story about two trick-or-treaters who were."

One Halloween two brothers went to a haunted house. It was the scariest one they had ever been through, and when they came out, they quietly peeked around the corner to see if anyone was following them. *(Draw from 1 to 2. This is the jack-o'-lantern's smile.)*

The boys were so sure they'd seen a ghost that they ran all the way around the block to get back to their apartment. *(Start at 3 and quickly draw around to point 4. This is the outline of half the jack-o'-lantern.)*

When they could see their apartment building, the brothers did not feel quite so scared, so they slowed down and just walked the rest of the way home. *(Slowly finish drawing the jack-o'-lantern from 4 up to 3.)*

Just then, in front of their building, the boys saw that someone had spilled a bag of nacho chips. *(Draw triangles 5, 6, and 7. These are the eyes and nose.)*

The brothers decided to clean up the mess. Just as they were throwing away the trash, they saw an empty box next to the dumpster. *(Draw line 8. This is the stem.)* Do you know what was in it? *(Listeners probably will answer "a pumpkin" or "a jack-o'-lantern.")*

Well . . . those two brothers looked in the box *(Very slowly remove the tape that holds the drawing closed.),* and they saw a . . . *(Remove paper from chalkboard and open it out with a flair.)* GHOST.

Optional Activities

1. What else could the brothers have seen in the box?

2. Could you make up a scary story that happens on Halloween?

3. Have you ever picked up someone else's trash? If we all picked up trash when we saw it, how would that improve our environment?

> **To make Halloween Scare:** *Use one sheet of paper, drawing the ghost on one side and the pumpkin face on the other. Fold paper from sides to cover the ghost and make the pumpkin face. Draw patterns with top and bottom matches as shown.*

Fold Line

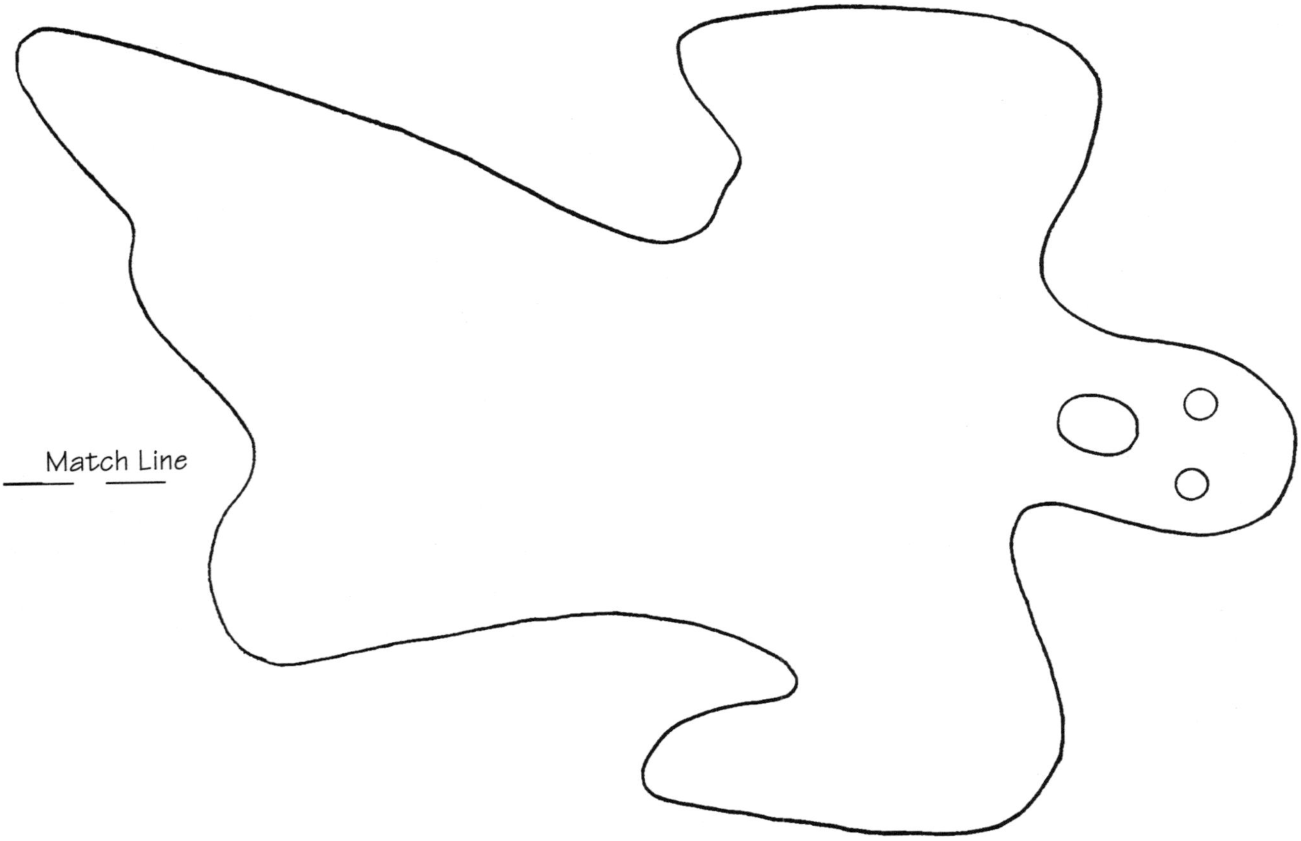

Match Line

Tape

Tape

Fold Line

Lost in the Mountains

Prefold paper and tape to a hard surface. Use a green marker on white paper.

Optional introductory statement: "This is a story about two brothers who figured out a way to solve a problem."

Once upon a time there were two brothers, Grant and Jordan. They had taken a walk in the mountains and got lost. They climbed up and down several mountains looking for a path out. **(Draw up and down from 1 through 8.)** When they got to the top of the highest mountain, Grant looked down and saw something shiny laying on a path below.

"Let's go see what that shiny thing is," said Jordan.

They quickly ran down the mountain and around the lake. **(Draw from 8 to 9 to 10, then draw oval A. This is the lake.)**

They ran all the way around the lake on a winding path until they came to the shiny object. **(Draw from 10 to 11 to 12, then back to 1 as you tell this.)**

Can you guess what was laying in the path? **(Pause and allow listeners to answer.)** Yes, it was a SAW. But how could this help them find their way out of the mountains?

As they turned the saw over and over in their hands **(Untape and turn the paper over and around several times.)**, they noticed that it glinted in the sun. In fact, remember that's how they found it in the first place!

Then Jordan had an idea. **(Retape the paper on the hard surface upside down.)** "Let's retrace our steps and climb to the top of the highest mountain again. There we can flash the shiny saw back and forth in the sunlight, and maybe someone will notice us."

So they took off down the winding path again **(Draw from 1 to 13 to 14.)**, past the lake **(Draw oval B, then draw from 14 to 15 to 16.)**, and then to the top of the tallest mountain. **(Draw from 16 to 17.)**

As they waved the saw so it could catch the light, off in the distance they heard an answering call. Quickly they ran up and down all the mountains like steps until they came to the top of the first mountain they had climbed. **(Draw up and down from 17 to 23.)**

When they got there, do you know what they found? **(Quickly connect 23 to 1. Untape the paper, fold the edges to cover up the saws, and turn to show the tree.)**

Yes, they found a TALL TREE. At the top of this tree was their friend Andrew, who had come to look for them. Andrew waved and yelled to the boys. "Stay where you are. Keep flashing your saw at me. I'll be right down."

With the help of the saw **(Fold paper to the center match line and show just one saw.)**, the tree **(Show tree.)**, and Andrew, Grant and Jordan were not lost anymore!

Optional Activities

1. What do you know about Morse code?
2. Try communicating by flashing aluminum pie pans in the sun back and forth at a partner.
3. Discuss safety when hiking, what to do if you get lost, etc.

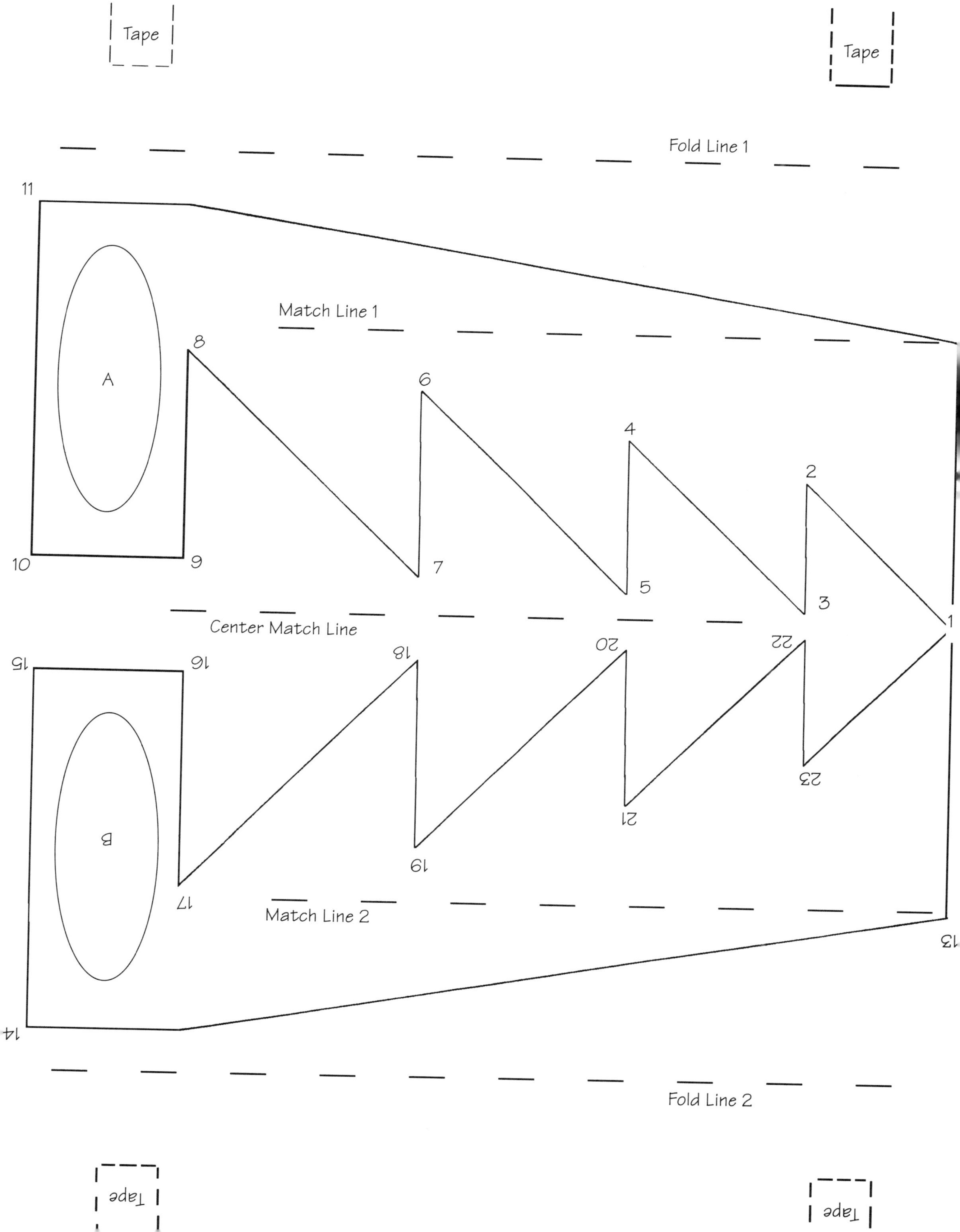

Tape

Tape

Fold Line 1

11

A

Match Line 1

8

6

4

2

7

5

3

10   9

1

Center Match Line

15   16

18

20

22

23

B

17

19

21

Match Line 2

14

13

Fold Line 2

Tape

Tape

No Water—No Legs

Prefold paper and tape to a hard surface.

Optional introductory statement: *"Here's a tale about something very strange that happened to an animal many years ago."*

Once upon a time, a long time ago, there was a summer, a hot, dry, no-rain summer. And on all the trees, the leaves dried up and fell off their branches. *(In the center of the page, draw a tall cylindrical "trunk" and add a series of "branches," each slightly bent upward and increasingly longer toward the bottom of the trunk.)* The branches all were bare.

The birds who lived in the trees were miserable sitting on these bare branches. *(Draw a short thick vertical line at the end of each branch.)* They had no shade from the hot sun, and they missed the delicious bugs that used to crawl on the cool, moist leaves.

These birds had flown everywhere to look for water *(Continue drawing birds at the end of every branch.)*, but there wasn't any. They decided to ask a fellow animal for help. Can you tell whom they asked? *(Quickly draw two small circles for eyes at the top of the trunk, then untape and rotate the page.)* Yes, it was a CENTIPEDE!

The birds on the branches said *(Turn the paper to show the tree again, and point out the birds.)*, "Friend centipede, we don't have any water. Could you please crawl down under the rocks and in the caves, to places where only you can go, and bring us some water? We know those dark hidden places have water. The hot sun cannot reach there to take it away."

The centipede snarled *(Turn the paper to show the centipede.)*, "No, I'll not get you water. Maybe it will rain someday." He snickered and walked off. *(Make centipede "walk" away.)*

The birds *(Turn the paper upright again.)* called after him, "Oh, but please, we need water. Only you can help us. Animals of the earth are supposed to help each other. We'll help you if you ever need it. Please!"

But the centipede hid under a large rock that sheltered a cool puddle of water. *(Show the centipede again.)* So the birds decided the only thing to do was to ask the Spirit of the Earth for help. They all prayed, "Oh Earth Spirit, we need water. We asked our fellow animal, the centipede, for help but he refused. Please send us a big rain."

The next day there was a big rain. It filled up the rivers and ponds again. All the birds had a big drink. And they twittered and chirped their thanks to the Earth Spirit.

But the Earth Spirit did one other thing. He found that centipede *(Show centipede.)* hiding under his big rock, and asked, "Why did you not help your fellow animals, the birds?"

The centipede started to whine, "Well, they get to fly. They can go anywhere they want. They have wings and all I have are so many of these skinny legs and feet. I have to walk everywhere. I'm tired of moving all these feet and legs around."

No sooner had the centipede said that, than the Earth Spirit zapped him! You know what he did to that centipede? *(Fold in both sides of the paper, to cover the centipede's legs. Pause while showing listeners.)* Yes, he turned the centipede into a . . . WORM! That's why worms don't have legs today and why they are always hiding from birds! *(If a listener suggests a snake, slug, or other animal that doesn't have legs, accept this answer and adapt the last sentence accordingly.)*

Optional Activities

1. There are many stories that explain how an animal became the way he is today. You can locate some others in the library.

2. Discuss the difference between reality and make-believe. What parts of this story could really happen?

3. Not having enough water can be a problem in many parts of our country. What can we do to help conserve water?

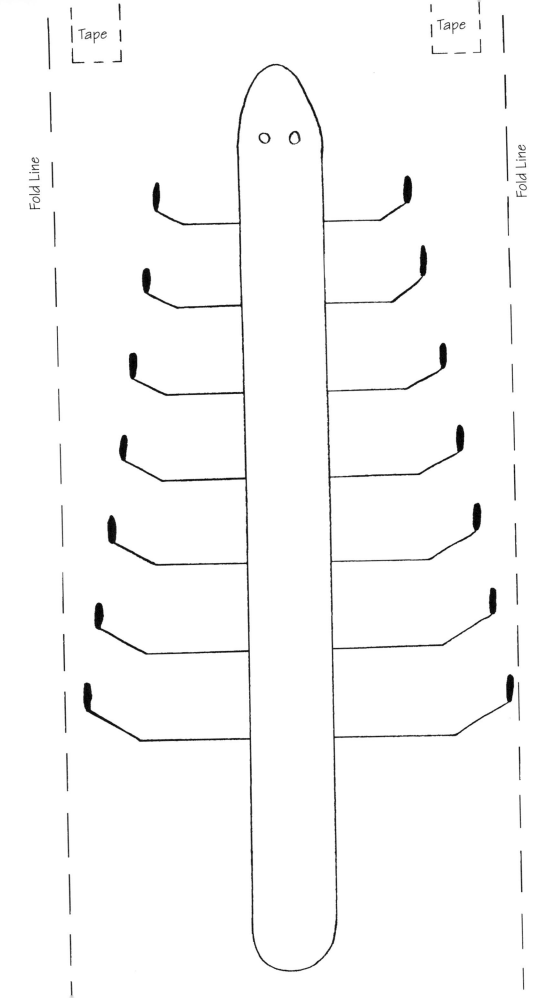

Tape

Tape

Fold Line

Fold Line

Ladybugs

Prefold paper. Draw the outside lines with a green marker. You will also need a black and a red marker. Tape the paper, inside the fold lines, to a hard surface.

Optional introductory statement: "How many of you have ever seen a ladybug? (Pause.) Here are some interesting facts about them."

People believe that if a ladybug lands on you, you will have good luck. Some people even make a wish quickly before the ladybug flies off again.

As you know, a ladybug has a hard shell that is red. (***Draw the outside shell line with a green marker, then color in the shell with a red marker.***) The red shell has black spots on it. (***Color in 11 black spots.***)

The ladybug's head is rather small. (***Draw the head.***) On its head are two antennae that help it smell and touch. (***Draw the antennae.***) The ladybug also has compound eyes, which means they're made up of many lenses. (***Draw circles for eyes, and dot in several "lenses."***)

A ladybug has two ways to protect itself. If frightened, a ladybug will fold up its legs and head inside its hard shell and pretend to be dead. When a bird or other insect wants to eat a ladybug, it will squirt a bad-tasting orange liquid out of its legs. (***Draw legs on the left side along with some droplets.***) The liquid tastes so terrible that the bird spits out the ladybug and stays away from all other ladybugs.

When the ladybug starts to fly, the shell separates and lifts. The wings unfold and off the ladybug goes. (***Open up the paper and draw the wings.***) When the ladybug lands, it folds its wings and protects them neatly under the wing covers. (***Fold the paper closed again.***)

The ladybug's favorite food is a small green bug called an "aphid." An aphid can kill flowers and garden plants by sucking out all their juices. One ladybug can eat 500 aphids a day, so farmers sometimes buy ladybugs by the boxful to put in their gardens in the spring. These ladybugs can save a large garden from being eaten by aphids.

The next time a ladybug lands on you, make a wish and gently put it in your garden. You might just save one of your favorite summertime snacks from being eaten by aphids. (***Untape the paper, hold the ladybug facing you, and unfold the right side out, showing the watermelon slice.***)

Do you know what food this is? Yes! It's a WATERMELON!

Optional Activities

1. Have you ever grown anything in a flowerpot or garden? What kinds of seeds would you like to plant in a garden or flower bed?

2. Find out more about ladybugs, aphids, and other insects.

3. What fresh fruits and vegetables do you like to eat in the summer?

To make the Ladybug: *Use one sheet of paper, drawing the wings on one side and the body on the other. Fold paper from sides to make the lady bug. Draw patterns with top and bottom matches as shown.*

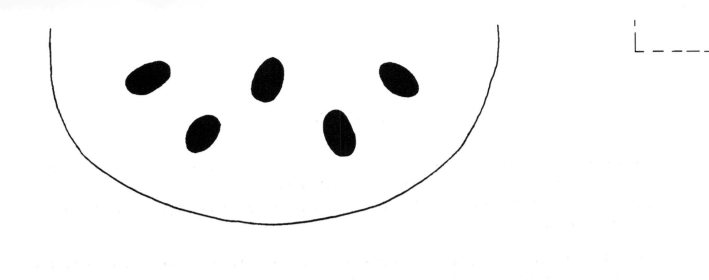

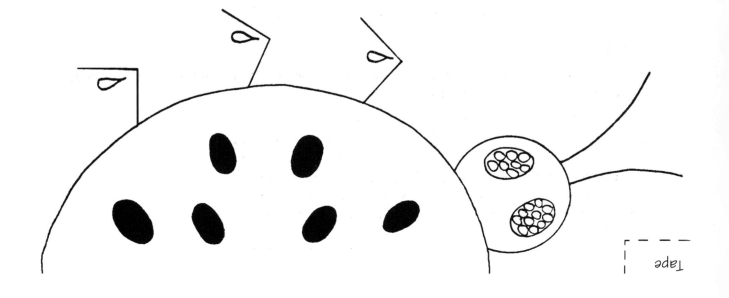

Fairies

Prefold paper and tape to a hard surface.

Optional introductory statement: "Lots of people believe in fairies, but not many know much about them. This is a story about fairies."

Not many people know this, but fairies did not always have wings and magic wands. They did have feet, though, really big feet. **(Draw the feet and the legs of fairy.)** They needed big feet! Fairies have lots of places to go in order to grant people's wishes. They have to go where the people are, you know, and sometimes need to walk across swamps, climb mountains, and walk down rocky hillsides. **(Draw the body and head as you say this.)**

The trouble was, walking took so long that often by the time the fairy arrived, the person making a wish was gone or didn't need it anymore. And with big feet, it was pretty hard to sneak under someone's pillow to get their tooth without waking them up. Worse than than, it was really hard to walk across a birthday cake to grant a wish and not leave big footprints in the icing.

So fairies with big feet just didn't work! You know what they decided they needed? **(Pause.)** Yes! WINGS! **(Fold flap over feet and draw wings.)**

Wings worked out much better. Now the fairies could fly around granting their magic wishes. And you've never seen any footprints on your birthday cake, have you?

Although wings did make life easier, fairies still had one small difficulty to work out. Fairies used to just throw wishes at people. But sometimes their aim wasn't very good and a tree could end up wearing a beautiful dress for a dance! **(Draw the fairy's arm and hand.)**

To fix this, the fairies decided to wrap each wish around a rock and then throw it at the wisher. This was a great system; the wishes got there every time. **(Draw a rock in the hand.)** But people didn't like getting hit with a rock, even if it did have their wish around it!

So, the fairies decided rocks wouldn't work for delivering wishes! They needed something else. Hmmm. Do you know what they decided on? **(Pause.)** Yes! A STICK with a STAR on the end of it. **(Fold the bottom flap up over the rock and draw a wand and star.)** Do you know what they called this? **(Pause.)** Yes! A MAGIC WAND. Now the wish could get there safely, and people love getting tapped by a star!

So that's why today fairies have wings instead of feet. **(Open the flap to show the feet again.)** And magic wands instead of rocks! **(Open the flap to show the rock again.)**

Optional Activities

1. How many different types of fairies do you know? Name some.

2. If you could have one wish granted by a fairy, what would it be? Tell a story about that.

3. Write a story about fairies—their favorite wish to grant, good fairies, bad fairies, tooth fairies (What do they do with all those teeth?), summer's night fairies, etc.

Tape

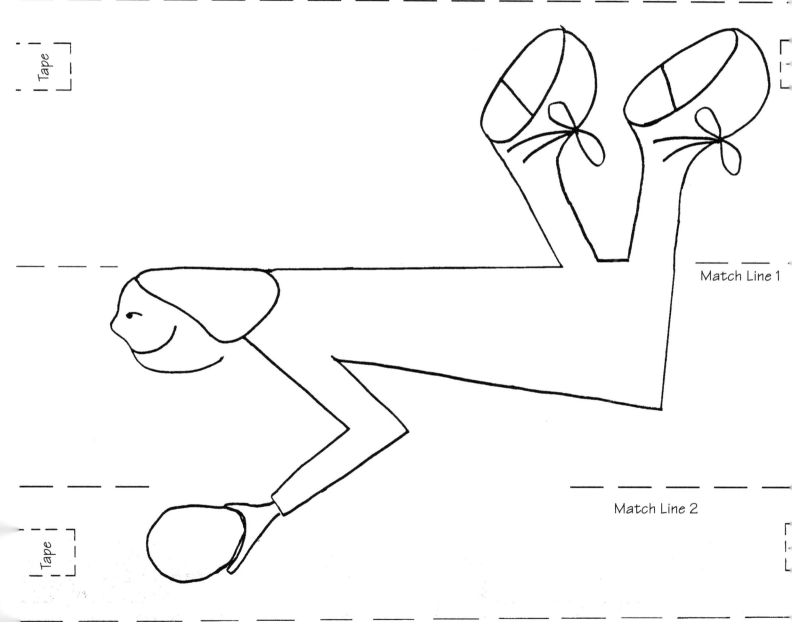

Match Line 1

Match Line 2

Tape

Fold Line 2

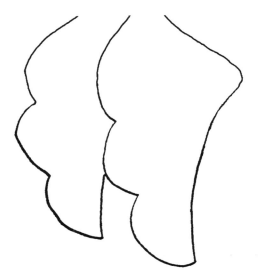

Other Folds

The Chase

Prefold paper and tape to a hard surface.

Optional introductory statement: *"This is a story about a boy who ran away from something, but he didn't know what!"*

Once there was a boy who loved to roller blade on his driveway. His driveway was especially good for this because it had a big curve. ***(Draw the bear's left ear.)***

His other favorite thing was to sit in the shade of his backyard between a big bush and some little ones. ***(Draw the bear's hair and fuzzy nose.)***

One day while he was sitting in the shade he thought he heard something up in the tree. It must be an animal—coming down to get him! He ran out of his yard and was so scared that he ran around his block. ***(Draw a line around from the bottom of the left ear to the bottom of the right ear. This is the bear's face.)***

When he got home ***(Draw the right ear.),*** he asked his mom if she saw anything. She said, "Well, I've been swinging in my hammock all afternoon." ***(Draw the smile.)***

"What do you think was chasing you? Was it a . . . BEAR?" ***(Draw both eyes. Show the drawing to your listeners, then fold up the bottom portion of the page and quickly draw an alligator nose and nostrils.)***

"Or was it an . . . ALLIGATOR?" ***(Again fold up the bottom portion of the page. This makes a double fold. This time draw a semicircle to complete the face, then a circle with two smaller circles in it for the pig's nose, and finish with a small mouth.)*** "Or was it a . . . PIG?"

Optional Activities

1. What are some other animals you could draw using the eyes and ears of the bear.

2. Tell a story about a time that you thought you were being chased by something. Were you scared?

3. Tell a story about what you would do if a bear or alligator were chasing you. Could a pig chase you?

Match Line

Fold Line 1

Fold Line 2

The Crayfish

Prefold and precut paper and tape to a hard surface.

Optional introductory statement: "There are many, many stories that explain why an animal is the way he is. Here is one of them."

If you go down this country road as far as you can *(Draw from 1 to 2.)* to the place where it curves around and doubles back on itself *(Draw from 2 around and back to 1.)*, you'll see the place where the crayfish live. *(Add eyes and legs.)*

Now everyone knows that crayfish have really short claws *(Draw short claws, line 3.)*, but not too many people know that once, long ago, *one* baby crayfish had very *long* claws. *(Draw long claws to end of paper, line 4.)* Here's the story my grandmother told me about that:

Junior Crayfish had really long claws *(Indicate drawing.)*, and he was so proud of them. He liked to wave them around in the air for everyone to see. He bragged about them and even polished them every night. But the worst of this behavior was that he was always sticking his claws where he wasn't supposed to.

One time he reached in through an open window and plucked a glass of lemonade right out of his grandfather's hand. Another time he reached over the back fence and pinched apples off his neighbor's tree. Everyone was getting tired of Junior Crayfish and his long claws.

His mama started to get on him about it. She said, "Now Junior, you've got to watch those claws. Don't you go and stick your claws out in the road."

Of course, that was the first thing that Junior did. He stuck his claws right out in the road. He thought he'd pinch himself a passing car. But do you know what happened? Instead of catching a car, a car got him! Now his claws weren't quite so long. *(Close flap A, and draw line 5.)*

Junior Crayfish didn't say much when his mama asked, "How is it that your claws are shorter this evening, Junior?"

The next day Mama Crayfish said, "Now Junior, you've got to watch those claws. Don't go and stick your claws down in the mud."

Of course, that was just the thing that Junior did. He went right to the biggest mudhole he could find and stuck his claws down in it just as far as he could. *(Pause.)* That wasn't too exciting, so he started to pull his claws out. But there they were—stuck. He pulled harder and harder. But do you know what happened? Yes! They broke off. *(Close flap B and draw line 6.)*

Junior Crayfish didn't say much when his mama asked, "How is it that your claws are shorter this evening, Junior?"

The next day Mama Crayfish said, "Now Junior, you've got to watch those claws. Don't you go and stick them up in a tree."

Of course, that was just the thing that Junior did. He went right to the tallest tree and stuck his claws up in it as far as he could. But do you know what happened? Yes! Junior's claws got stuck in that tree, and he had to pull and pull to get them unstuck! And they broke off some more! *(Close flap C.)*

Junior Crayfish didn't say much when his mama asked, "How is it that your claws are shorter this evening, Junior? Well, you know, now that I think about it, they look just about the same length as everyone else's claws."

And that is how Junior Crayfish ended up with short claws! At least—that's the way my grandmother always tells it.

Optional Activities

1. Discover more about crayfish and their habitat. How long are their claws?

2. There are lots of stories about animals and how they became the way they are. Perhaps you can find some in the library.

3. Can you choose an animal and think up an explanation about some part of it?

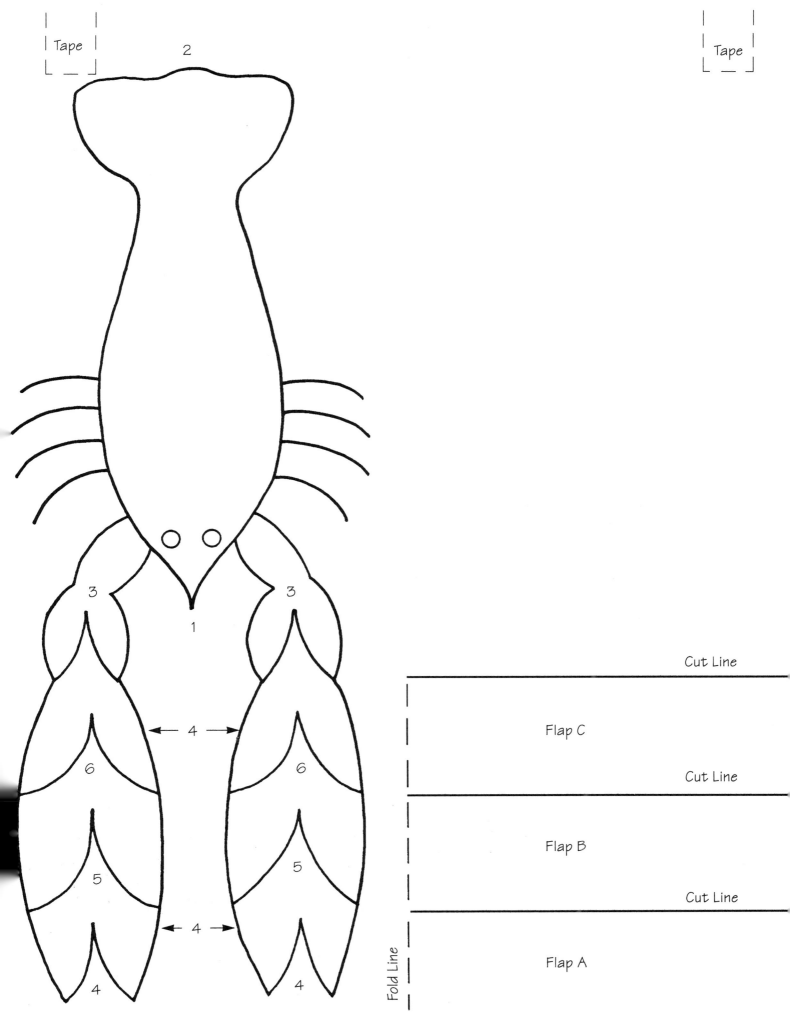

Tape

2

Tape

3

3

1

○ ○

4

6

6

5

5

4

4

Cut Line

Flap C

Cut Line

Flap B

Cut Line

Flap A

Fold Line

Going Home

Prefold paper and tape to a hard surface.

Optional introductory statement: "Have you ever been fishing? (Pause.) This is a story about going fishing."

One day two friends went out fishing together. They each had their own boat. ***(Draw left and right boats.)***

They each dropped a fishing line. ***(Draw lines down from boats.)***

They did not have to wait long before they each caught a fish. ***(Draw a fish at the bottom of the fishing lines on both sides of the paper.)***

Soon it was time to go home. One fisherman realized that his motor was out of gas, and he couldn't get home. He called over to his friend, "I'm out of gas. Can you give me a tow back to shore? It's too far to row all the way."

His friend answered, "Sure, row on over here." ***(Fold the right side of the paper over.)***

They hooked the two boats together. Then the other friend discovered that he was out of gas, too! The first friend was worried. "Oh no, what shall we do now?"

"Don't worry. I know another way to get back to shore," the second friend answered. "We can get home with this." ***(Fold the bottom section up, over the fish, and draw the sail. Turn the paper upside down to show the sailboat.)***

Do you know how they got home? Yes, they SAILED home! What did the fishing line turn out to be? Yes, the MAST for the sail.

Optional Activities

1. Tell about a time that you went fishing.
2. What else could you catch besides a fish? (This question can lead to some imaginative answers.)
3. How else could you get home if you could not use your motor?

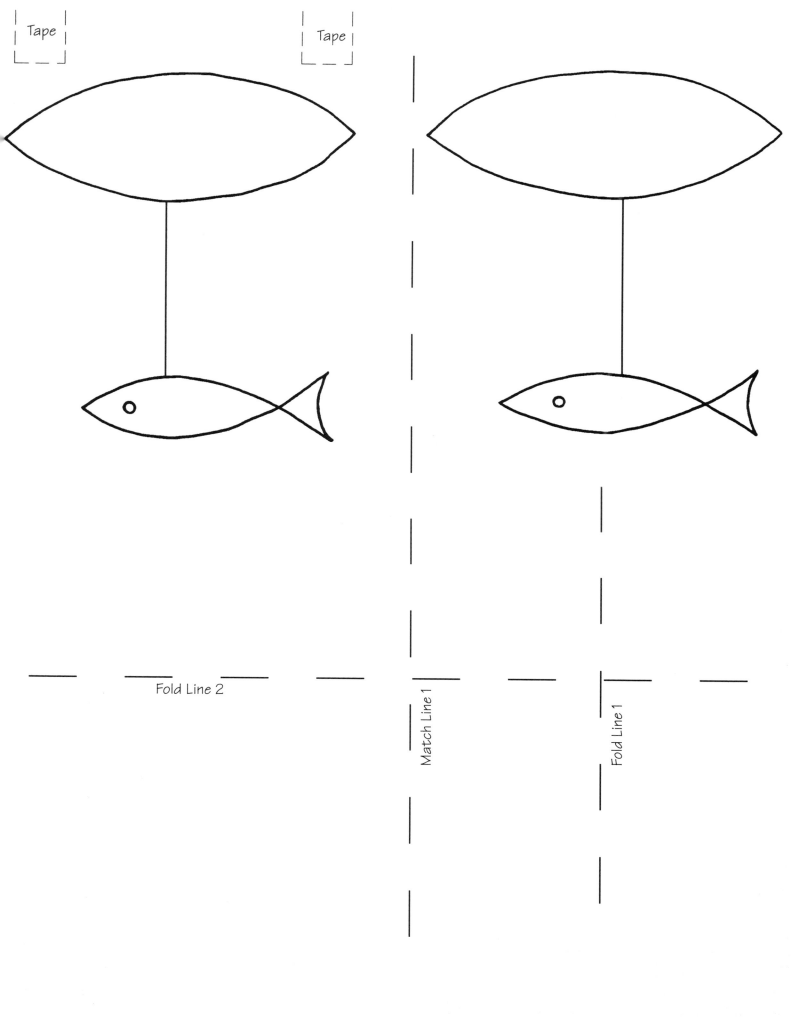

Tape

Tape

Fold Line 2

Match Line 1

Fold Line 1

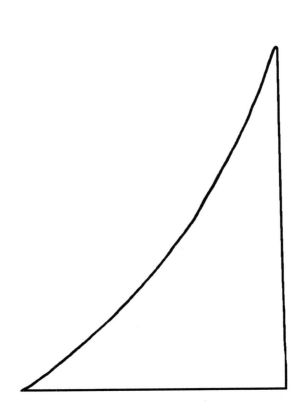

The Unhappy Office Building

This story has no folds. Tape paper to a hard surface.

Optional introductory statement: "Have you ever been in a very tall building? (Pause.) What is the tallest building around here?"

Once there was an office building that was not happy. *(Draw square 1.)* Even though it was so big that it had to be built on a special foundation, it was still not happy. *(Draw square 2.)*

This office building was such a busy place that more and more floors had to be added onto its top. *(Draw square 3 and pause. Then draw square 4 and pause. Then draw square 5.)*

With all these new top floors, this was now the tallest building in the city! Important people had their offices there. They held important meetings and made important decisions there. They made important telephone calls to other important people all over the world. In fact, they made so many important phone calls that two antennas had to be installed at the top of the building to send out all these calls. *(Draw lines 6 and 7.)* The antennas stuck up so high that now the office building could be seen from all over the city.

All these things should have made the unhappy office building happy, but they did not. The unhappy office building cried to itself, "I want people to come here to enjoy themselves, not just to work."

One day the man who had the top office got tired of everyone coming into his office just to look out his windows at the splendid view *(Draw squares 8 and 9.),* so he decided to build special windows for people to look out. *(Draw angles 10 and 11.)*

Now this made the unhappy office building a little happier. A lot of people were coming inside just to enjoy the view. But do you know what made the now not so unhappy office building the very happiest of all?

It was when the man in the top office decided to do something really special for the Fourth of July that year. He bought all the equipment he needed, and then, when it got dark, he shot fireworks, sparklers, and all kinds of rockets off the top of the building. *(Turn the paper upside down. Draw triangle 12.)*

Now the unhappy office building had become the Really Happy Office Building!

Optional Activities

1. Tell about a really fun Fourth of July you had. What did you do?
2. How do other people celebrate this holiday?
3. If you were designing a tall building, what would you put in it?

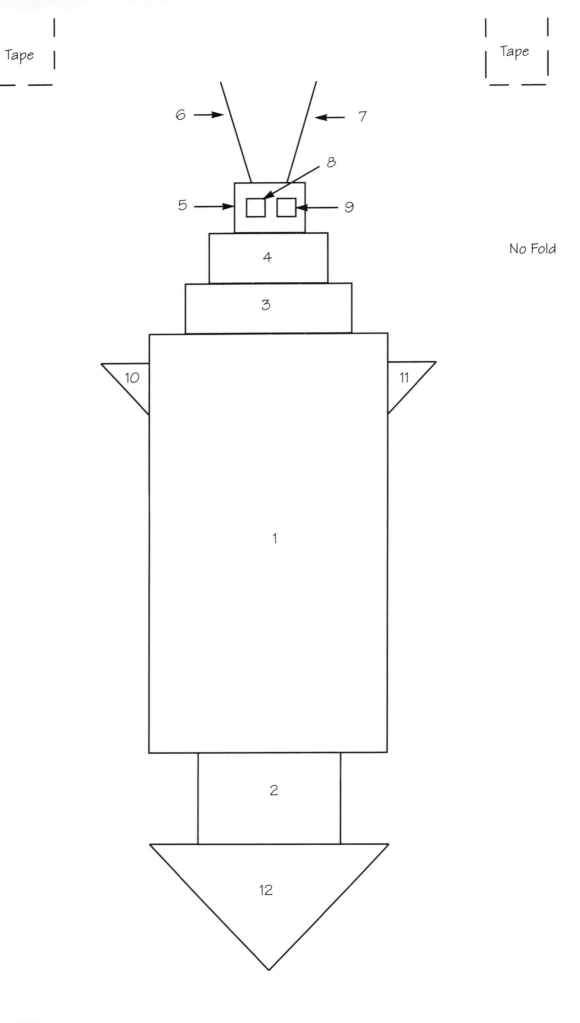

No Fold